ISBN-13: 978-1539677949
ISBN-10: 153967794X

To Amanda,

Words will never express my gratitude for all your support and love over the years, thank you for all you have taught me about being brave

Love Nicky
xx

Acknowledgements

Books are such special things, they have a magical ability to bury into our hearts and souls, allowing us to learn about things, places and ourselves. My love of books has been one which spans years, and some of my favourites still sit on my book shelf. My dream to create my own books has been a long one, but it wasn't until I found my destination that they came to life, and even then they sat in my imagination for so long. I am delighted to be able to create the Adventures of Brian and bring the magic of books and the wonders of therapeutic storytelling together to offer a combination of stories and support to children and their families. Before we start this special story there is thanks to be given;

To my Mum and Dad, who have given me the encouragement to move forward with a dream of creating stories to help small people. Thank you for standing by me, encouraging me and sharing these precious moments.

To Richard for your belief and encouragement that there was a set of books inside me that should be written, this shiny diamond is very grateful.

To my nan and granddad, who forever guide me to follow this path that I am on and to ensure that I stay true to my dreams.

To Veronica, thank you for allowing me the privilege of naming Brian after Brian. There is a sprinkling of him all over this book.

To Elise, Darcey & Boo, thank you for your ongoing love and support. For sharing our memories and mostly for sharing these stories as each one unfolds.

To Amanda, thank you for your unwavering faith in me and the endless love and support you have given from day one of our friendship. You are one of the bravest lady's I know.

I hope you enjoy these books as much as I have enjoyed writing them

Love Nicky x x

THE ADVENTURES OF BRIAN

HELPING CHILDREN OVERCOME THEIR FEARS AND WORRIES

This book belongs to:

....

One morning Brian was out walking in the sunshine with his mummy. Brian loved to go walking, he enjoyed sniffing the flowers and rolling in the grass. Brian especially loved this because it meant that he got to say hello to all his neighbours and sometimes they gave him cuddles.

Brian was walking along enjoying sniffing a lamp-post when all of a sudden he STOPPED!

"Come on Brian" his mummy said.

Brian didn't move. He was frozen to the spot!

Up ahead he could see something....

It was a BIG BLACK DOG!

"What's the matter Brian?" his mummy said kneeling down beside him.

Brian hid behind his mummy – he peered around her legs and looked at the Big Black Dog ahead of him….

The Big Black Dog looked at Brian and Brian looked at the Big Black Dog.

Brian looked all around him for a better place to hide, he saw a big tree so ran over to it and hid behind it dragging his mummy with him!

"Don't you want to say hello?" his mummy asked him

Brian ran further behind the tree, hoping that the Big Black Dog could not see him!

"Oh Brian" his mummy said….and started walking back toward their home.

Brian walked as quickly as he could to get away!

When they got home Brian ran out in the garden hoping that his friend the Blue Butterfly would be there.

Brian ran out in the garden and sat on her flower was the Blue Butterfly.

"Oh Blue Butterfly, I am so glad to see you!" Brian yelled as he ran towards her.

Blue Butterfly looked up from her flower and stared at Brian. "Hello Brian, are you ok?" she asked.

"Oh Blue Butterfly, I was so scared!" Brian exclaimed.

"Brian what happened? Tell me all about it?" Blue Butterfly said.

Brian settled down on the grass next to Blue Butterfly's flower and started to tell her about his morning walk.

"It was so lovely Blue Butterfly. Until we saw the Big Black Dog!" he told her.

"What's wrong with the Big Black Dog?" Blue Butterfly asked. Brian sat up a little bit, his eyes grew wider and then he started to tell her…. "It was so big! Its paws were huge! Its head was the size of the moon! I was so scared Blue Butterfly"

Blue Butterfly was silent for a moment and then she said "Brian, did it growl at you?"

Brian sat for a moment and then very quietly said "No".

"Did it bark at you Brian?" Blue Butterfly asked. Brian looked at the floor…. "No" he whispered.

"Hmm, did he push you Brian?" Blue Butterfly asked.

Brian looked up at Blue Butterfly and replied "No".

"So the Big Black Dog was bigger than you, but it didn't bark, it didn't growl and it didn't push you?" Blue Butterfly asked him. Brian was quiet for a moment whilst he thought and then said "No Blue Butterfly, he didn't bark at me, he didn't growl at me and he didn't push me".

"So why were you scared of the Big Black Dog Brian?" Blue Butterfly asked him.

"It was huge!" Brian replied!

Blue Butterfly spread her wings and made herself more comfortable on her flower before she said…. "Brian, just because it is bigger than you doesn't mean it will hurt you. It's just new!"

Brian looked surprised "New?" he echoed. Blue Butterfly smiled, "Yes Brian…. it's something that you haven't seen before. Sometimes, when we see things that are different it can scare us. Just think for a moment, you don't feel scared when you see Boo do you?"

Brian thought about all the happy things he did with Boo, like running around the garden and playing in the field…. "No, I am not scared of Boo, she is my friend" he replied.

"So, when you play with Boo you have fun, but when you saw the Big Black Dog you were scared, just because it was bigger?" Blue Butterfly asked him.

Brian thought about what Blue Butterfly had said…. When he thought about it she was right. Boo and the Big Black Dog were both dogs…. "I do have lots of fun with Boo" he whispered.

"Well, the Big Black Dog has a name too and if you think about it you might find that really he is just a bigger version of Boo. You could even find that you really like him if you got to know him" Blue Butterfly explained.

Brian thought about this…. He wasn't sure about Boo when he first met her, in fact he had hidden behind his mummy to get away from her! BUT… when he spent time with her and got to know her he found that he really liked her…. In fact, now they are best friends! So maybe, the sooner he spent time with the Big Black Dog then the sooner they could become friends too….

"Do you know a really good way to find out if a dog is friendly Brian?" Blue Butterfly asked him. Brian shook his head.

"Well Brian, an easy way to tell if a dog is friendly is to wiggle your tail at it!"

Brian looked at Blue Butterfly and then asked "Wiggle my tail?"

"Yes, if you wiggle your tail at the dog and it wiggles its tail back then you know that it would like to play!" Blue Butterfly told him. Brian liked this idea.... Maybe he could try this.

The next day Brian was out walking with his mummy. He was sniffing the flowers when he saw the Big Black Dog up ahead. He froze to the spot...... He looked at the Big Black Dog and the Big Black Dog looked at him.

Then he remembered what the Blue Butterfly had said to him.... "If you got to know him then you may find that you like him, couldn't you?" He thought about it and decided that she was right.

So he slowed down and looked at the Big Black Dog.... Its paws were very big! Its head was still as big as the moon, and from way down here it was a lot bigger than him....

Brian took a big breath and he looked at the Big Black Dog and then he wiggled his tail to tell him that he was friendly.... And he waited....

He smiled and stood looking at the Big Black Dog and he waited. Then all of a sudden the Big Black Dog wiggled his tail back! He was friendly too! Brian was so excited!

Now Brian knew that the Big Black Dog was friendly he felt a little bit better, so very slowly Brian wandered a little bit closer... after all, he was very small compared to the Big Black Dog and he knew that you should never run towards other dogs as it can scare them.

"Hello!" the Big Black Dog said in his deep voice.

"Hello! I'm Brian" Brian said in his little voice.

"I'm Keizer! You are very small!" the Big Black Dog replied.

"Well you are very big!" Brian said to him

Keizer laughed, "Perhaps we can be friends though? I like little dogs!" Keizer told him

Brian thought about it, it might be nice to have a new friend... and Keizer was very nice! He wiggled his tail... "Deal, let's be friends!"

Brian and Keizer walked along the path together and smelt the grass and looked at the flowers. Brian looked at Keizer and smiled, now he had gotten to know him he realised that when you take your time to say hello sometimes the dogs that scare us are not scary at all!

Keizer looked at Brian "What are you thinking about Brian?" he asked.

"I thought you were really scary" Brian admitted.

"Shall I tell you a secret?" Keizer asked him.

"A secret.....ooo ok!" Brian replied eagerly.

"I was a little bit scared of you too!" Keizer admitted to him.

"You were scared of me?" Brian asked, he was very surprised.

"Yes, sometimes little dogs are scary when you are so big!" Keizer told him.

Brian had never considered that Keizer could be scared of him too. Then, when he thought about it, sometimes even humans were a little bit scary especially when they lent down over him with their big hands! He didn't think they realised that they were so big compared to him!

"How did you decide that I was friendly?" he asked Keizer.

"When you wiggled your tail at me to say hello I knew that you were nice!" Keizer said to him.

Brian smiled, Blue Butterfly was right, looking for wiggly tails was a good way to tell that a dog was friendly!

Brian snuggled into Keizer and said "I'm glad that you decided you liked me"

Keizer looked down at Brian and replied "Me too, now we can be friends too!". Then they wandered along the path together sniffing the flowers.

The next day Brian was playing with his ball in the garden when Blue Butterfly fluttered over and landed on his head! Brian giggled "What are you doing?" Brian asked her.

"Just watching you" Blue Butterfly giggled then floated down onto her flower. Brian sat down next to her and looked at her closely.

"So, how was Keizer?" Blue Butterfly asked.

Brian smiled, "Keizer is really nice! You probably already know, but when you take your time to get to know dogs some of them are really nice!".

"Yes Brian, you are right! When you take your time and check that a dog is friendly then you can get to know each other and become friends!" Blue Butterfly said.

Brian remembered the lovely walk that he had had with Keizer. "When I took my time, and we wiggled our tails and walked up to each other slowly I could tell that he was friendly too!"

Blue Butterfly looked at Brian and smiled. "Brian I am so proud of you!"

Brian looked up at Blue Butterfly and grinned 'Why are you proud of me?"

"Brian, when you took your time to say hello to Keizer and got to know him you realised that he was nice and you made a new friend. I am really proud of you" Blue Butterfly explained to him.

Brian thought about it, one of the things that he loved about getting to know Keizer was that he made a new friend and that Blue Butterfly was proud of him. "Thank you for teaching me how to make friends with new dogs Blue Butterfly" Brian said to her.

"Just remember, when you meet a new dog you just need to look at their tail, check that they are friendly and if you go to say hello walk up slowly" Blue Butterfly replied.

"I can check with my mummy too!" Brain said.

"Yes, we can check with our mummies and also the mummy or daddy of the dog too" Blue Butterfly replied. From that day on Brian remembered to always check tails (and with his mummy) and he made lots of new friends.

Nicky lives in Sussex with Brian the Cockapoo where they enjoy daily adventures with friends and family. Nicky started her career by spending 10 years working in the early years sector with 0-5 year olds before lecturing in early years and health and social care to students aged 16 and over. She later retrained as a hypnotherapist and now runs A Step at a Time Hypnotherapy working with children and adults to resolve their personal issues.

The Adventures of Brian books were the development of a dream of wanting to offer parents of young children tools and resources to support their children to manage worries and fears in a non-intrusive way. Having spent a large part of her career reading stories at all speeds and in all voices this collection of storybooks was born.

Each book in the collection covers a different worry which affects children on a day to day basis and uses therapeutic storytelling to support children in resolving these through Brian's daily adventures.

You can find more titles in the Adventures of Brian series by visiting:

www.adventuresofbrian.co.uk

Printed in Great Britain
by Amazon